The Mouse Who Saved Egypt

Karim Alrawi *illustrated by* Bee Willey

TRADEWIND BOOKS

VANCOUVER • LONDON

To Adam the artist—KA • *For Herman, John O and John S, with a debt of gratitude—BW*

Published
by Tradewind
Books in 2011

Text copyright © 2011
Karim Alrawi
Illustrations copyright ©
2011 Bee Willey

LIBRARY AND ARCHIVES CANADA CATALOGUING IN PUBLICATION

Alrawi, Karim, 1952-
The mouse who saved Egypt / Karim Alrawi ; illustrated
by Bee Willey.

ISBN 978-1-896580-79-1

1. Mice--Juvenile fiction. 2. Egypt--Juvenile fiction.
I. Willey, Bee, 1963- II. Title.

PR6051.L6M68 2010   j823'.914   C2010-902917-8

CATALOGUING AND PUBLICATION DATA AVAILABLE FROM THE BRITISH LIBRARY.

Book design by Elisa Gutiérrez   The text of this book is set in Archer

10 9 8 7 6 5 4 3 2 1   Printed in Singapore on FSC paper April 2011 by Tien Wah Press

FSC
Mixed Sources
Cert no. SW-COC-001271
© 1996 FSC

The publisher thanks the Government of Canada and Canadian Heritage for their financial support
through the Canada Council for the Arts, the Canada Book Fund and Livres Canada Books. The publisher
also thanks the Government of the Province of British Columbia
for the financial support it has given through the Book Publishing
Tax Credit program and the British Columbia Arts Council.

Canada Council
for the Arts

Conseil des Arts
du Canada

BRITISH
COLUMBIA
ARTS COUNCIL

One evening, a young Egyptian prince saw a mouse caught in the thorns of a bush.

"Please kind sir help me," the mouse squeaked. "If you don't, the jackals will surely eat me."

The prince felt sorry for the mouse and set him free.

"True greatness is being kind, and true kindness is never forgotten," said the mouse, scurrying away across the sand.

T he young prince dreamed that the sun god spoke to him:

I, Amon-Ra, give life to this land,
Yet my image lies buried deep in the sand.
Neglected, forgotten, banished from sight,
I'll make him pharaoh who brings it to light.

When the prince awoke, he realized what the sun god's words meant.

On returning to the palace, the young prince ordered his workmen to clear away the sand around the great rock. Toiling day and night, they uncovered a giant stone sphinx, part man and part lion—the sacred image of the sun god, Ra.

When the old pharaoh died, the high priest sent for the prince.

"For every sun that sets, a new sun rises," he said. "It is the sun god's wish that you be crowned lord of the land."

That very day the prince was made pharaoh.

The young pharaoh ruled kindly, always mindful of the sun god's blessings.

The country prospered and the mice ate well.

One day, a messenger came to court. "A great army of mountain men is camped in the desert ready to attack," he said.

The sun god answered the pharaoh's prayers:

Every kind act is a seed sown.
Aiding others with their troubles
Reaps help with one's own.

The little mouse hurried to his friends. "The kind man who rescued me from the thorns needs our help," he said.

Thousands of mice set off across the desert. While the mountain men slept, the mice chewed through the leather of their bows, their saddles and the straps of their shields.

In the morning, the mountain men could not tie their sandals, and their clothes fell off. They could not saddle their horses, nor lift their shields, nor draw their bows. When they saw the pharaoh leading his soldiers, they fled.

At the foot of the sphinx, the young pharaoh built a temple to the sun god. Inside he placed a golden mouse to remind the people of Egypt that every act of kindness is rewarded—though sometimes in unexpected ways.